table for three

cm campbell

playlist

https://music.apple.com/us/playlist/table-for-three/pl.u-xlyNqMdCJ4vYKoW

dedication

For everybody who ever sat at Friendsgiving staring at that fine married couple like *damn… if they asked, I would absolutely ruin my life.*
This one's for you.

trigger warning

This story contains explicit adult content and mature themes that may not be suitable for all readers, including:

- Dominance and submission

- Praise kink and degradation

- Rough and messy sex

- Face-sitting and deep-throating

- Squirting and overstimulation

- Mutual masturbation and scissoring

- Public teasing and semi-public sexual play

- Spit play and breath play

- Voyeurism (including FaceTime-assisted scenes)

- Power exchange rooted in consent

- Intense emotional intimacy and possessiveness

- Polyamorous relationship dynamics (FFM)

synopsis

Last Thanksgiving changed everything.
Honesti crossed a line with the two people she's always
trusted most, then vanished before sunrise.
Now she's back in Atlanta for Friendsgiving, and the tension
hasn't gone anywhere. Symere and Maleia haven't forgotten.
Not her laugh, not that night, and definitely not the way she
left.
They're not mad. But they're not open-ended, either.
This Friendsgiving, everyone's getting stuffed.

prologue

. . .

The Night We Stopped Pretending

THANKSGIVING WASN'T SUPPOSED to end like this. Not with my face buried between Maleia's thighs and Symere driving himself into me like he's starving. But I guess some cravings don't belong at the dinner table. Until they do.

The house still smells like cinnamon yams, sage stuffing, and roasted turkey. The candles are low, the wine is mostly gone, and the playlist Symere queued up hours ago is looping back to something slow and sticky. They invited me over like they always do. But this time felt different. Maleia kept touching my hand when she passed me plates. Symere's eyes dragged when I laughed, when I crossed my legs, when I leaned over to grab the wine. I thought I was imagining it. Until I wasn't.

Now my dress is shoved up around my waist. My knees are slightly bent, legs parted, hips arched back over the edge of their dining table. My chest is pressed flat against the smooth wood, one cheek resting against it, lips parted and wet as I moan into the heat between Maleia's thighs.

She's perched at the edge of the table, leaning back on her hands, legs spread wide, and her heels dig into the groove of my shoulder blades as I eat her like a woman possessed.

She tastes like red wine and hunger. My tongue slides between her folds, slow and messy, tracing her clit before sucking it, hard and deliberate. Her thighs twitch every time I find the spot. Her hips roll with every pass of my tongue.

"God, baby," she gasps, fingers curling in my hair. "Don't stop. Just like that."

Behind me, Symere groans. His grip tightens around my waist as he thrusts into me again, burying himself deep. My mouth stutters on her pussy, and she moans louder, back arching, nails dragging down my scalp.

The rhythm of it all is sinful. His hips snapping against me in hard, punishing strokes. Her pussy grinding against my face. The air was thick with sweat, sex, and whatever line we crossed and never looked back.

"You see how she's takin' us?" Symere says, voice rough behind me. "Tongue in your pussy while this greedy little hole squeezes the life outta me."

I can't respond. My mouth is too full, my throat already raw from moaning against her. I flick my tongue over her clit in fast, tight circles. Her thighs clamp tighter, and she cries out.

"Fuck, H. That mouth should come with a warning."

He thrusts harder, deeper. Each slam jolts my body forward, grinding my face into Maleia's heat. I don't care. I want more. I curl two fingers inside her, hooking up as I suck and slide and take her apart from the inside out.

Maleia's close. I can feel it in the tremble of her legs, in the breathless way she says my name.

"You're gonna make me cum," she chokes out. "Don't stop. Oh my God, don't stop."

I don't. I flatten my tongue and let her ride it. Her whole body tightens, then breaks, thighs shaking, mouth falling open in a silent scream as she comes hard against my face. She's soaked, panting, voice gone. I don't stop licking until she twitches and pulls away, breath ragged, body boneless.

Symere slaps my ass with a grunt, then grabs my hips tighter and picks up the pace. He's slamming into me now. Fast. Vicious. My knees threaten to buckle, but he holds me steady, hips snapping into mine with the full weight of him.

"You wanted this, didn't you?" he growls. "Been walkin' around lookin' sweet, knowin' you'd bend over the second we touched you."

"Yes," I manage, voice wrecked. "Yes, please, Symere."

Maleia leans forward, hands on my back, then slides one down between my thighs. Her fingers rub tight, messy circles over my clit. I jerk at the contact. I'm already close. Too close.

"She's dripping," she whispers to him. "You feel how she's clenching around you?"

"Like a fucking vice," he hisses. "She gonna cum for us?"

"I want it," I beg, voice breaking. "Please, don't stop. I want all of it."

Symere fucks me harder, and Maleia keeps rubbing, whispering filth in my ear about how I look, how I taste, how they've both wanted me like this for months. I fall apart fast, no warning. My orgasm crashes through me, white-hot and blinding, and I scream into the table as my whole body locks up.

Symere groans behind me, grips me hard, and pumps into me deep one last time as he spills inside me, hot and thick and endless. His body shakes against mine. His breath is hot on my back.

For a long moment, we don't move.

Just gasps. Sweaty skin. The sound of Maleia's soft laughter as she strokes my back.

Symere pulls out slowly. I feel the warmth of him dripping down my thigh. Maleia presses a kiss between my shoulders.

"You good, baby?" she asks gently.

I nod, still trembling. My legs don't work yet.

Symere lifts me like I don't weigh anything. His arms are solid, sure, as he carries me to their bathroom. Maleia follows, brushing my hair back, her voice soft.

The shower is hot and slow. Their hands are all over me, washing, caressing, teasing again, but not with the same urgency. Just intimacy. Warmth. Reverence. We don't talk much. We don't need to. They take care of me like I belong here. Like I'm more than a body they borrowed for the night.

When we finally crawl into bed, the sheets are fresh and cool. Symere curls behind me. Maleia presses into my front, her fingers lacing with mine under the covers. I'm floating, somewhere between wrecked and weightless, and the heat of their bodies keeps me grounded.

Nobody says a word.

And I fall asleep thinking maybe, just maybe, I was always meant to be right here.

———

I wake up to silence. The kind that presses in too thick, too still. The kind that doesn't belong to me.

Symere's chest is warm against my back. Maleia's thigh is draped over mine, her breath slow and steady against my shoulder. We're a tangle of limbs and sheets, our bodies still slick with the memory of last night. For a minute, I just stare at the ceiling, letting the panic sink its teeth in.

What the fuck did I just do?

They're married. I'm their best friend. This wasn't supposed to happen, and yet it did. I wanted it. I begged for it. But now that the fog is lifting, all I can feel is the weight of it pressing down on my chest.

What happens now? Do we talk about it over coffee and leftover pie? Do I pretend like it didn't mean something when I know it did?

Slowly, I shift my body away from theirs. I move like a thief, careful not to wake them. Maleia sighs in her sleep, nuzzling into the sheets. Symere's arm falls into the space I leave behind. The absence of their touch makes everything feel colder.

I make my way to the bathroom. My reflection in the mirror is a mess-eyes tired, mouth swollen, hair wild. I wash up. Rinse my mouth. Pull my curls back into a puff. The room still smells like them. Like us.

In the bedroom, I gather my clothes from the floor. Bra. Panties. Dress. Shoes. I get dressed slowly, feeling every piece slide over skin that still remembers their hands. My thighs ache. My lips are tender. Faint marks are blooming along my hips. I touch them and wonder what the hell I was thinking.

Before I go, I clean up. The dining room still has the ghost of last night lingering around it. I wipe down the table. Gather plates. Toss away the candles that have burned out. I move quietly, mechanically, like doing something useful will make this feel less messy inside me.

The sun is creeping in through the windows when I stop by the kitchen counter. I find a pen and a sticky note beside a grocery list. My hand shakes a little as I write.

I'm sorry. I just need some time to think. I love you both, and I promise I'll call soon.

I stare at it for a few seconds before sticking it on the fridge, right next to a magnet shaped like a peach and a takeout menu. It looks too small for what I'm feeling, but I don't know how to say any of this out loud.

I take one last look around their house. Our mess is gone, but the air still feels charged. I press my lips together, grab my keys, and slip out into the morning.

The cold hits me harder than I expect. I don't bother with a coat. I just keep walking to my car, one step at a time, hoping the ache in my chest will fade with the miles.

Hoping I didn't just ruin the best thing I never saw coming.

one

. . .

Don't Run From What Wants You

THE AUTOMATIC DOORS part and the air outside Atlanta's airport hits me like memory, thick, humid, and familiar enough to make my chest tighten. I drag my carry-on behind me, scanning the line of parked cars until I see him.

Symere.

Leaning against the black SUV like he owns the damn lot, one hand tucked in his pocket, the other gripping the edge of the hood. Grey joggers sitting right on his hips, dick print bold enough to make my mouth go dry. Black Henley stretched across his chest and arms like it was made for him. Beard trimmed clean, gold chain catching the late sun. He looks good, too good. Like time's been treating him good. Like he ain't missed a beat.

And I feel every second of that night again.

His hands on me. My lips on her. His voice in my ear. Her fingers in my hair. Our breath mixing with the scent of roasted turkey and cinnamon candles. The way they held me after. Like I belonged. And the way I disappeared the next morning.

My steps slow, but not because I'm hesitant. More like I'm soaking in the sight of him. The weight of everything we didn't say this past year sits low in my belly. We've talked, little texts, random check-ins, stupid jokes that made me blush in the middle of the day, but we never talked about *that* night. Never opened that door again.

Until now.

He sees me. And his whole face shifts, like the grin was already waiting, just needed me to unlock it.

"There she go," he says, voice low and warm. "Little rabbit, finally stopped runnin'."

The nickname makes my breath catch. I walk closer. "Happy Thanksgiving to you, too and I wasn't running."

He straightens up, eyes dragging over me slow, like he's checking for damage. "Happy Thanksgiving. You left a note, H. A whole damn note."

I reach him. He steps into my space without hesitation, fingers brushing a curl back from my face, then drifting down to catch my chin. He lifts it until I'm looking right at him.

"You look good," he says. "But I need you to hear me, real clear. We ain't mad. Not me, not Maleia. We both want you here. But this ain't a game. If you still unsure, or if you think you might disappear again, then this can't be anything more than friends. We can't do history on repeat."

My breath shudders. "I'm not running this time."

"Then say that with your chest," he murmurs. His hand stays on my chin, thumb brushing soft over my bottom lip.

I exhale through my nose. "I'm here. For real."

"Good," he says. Then he leans in. Not too close, just enough for his lips to graze the shell of my ear. "Been waitin' to see if you was gon' come back and act like you never left."

His hand slides around my waist, fingers firm and warm through my hoodie. He tugs me in until we're chest to chest. My heart's racing.

"You still soft everywhere I remember," he whispers, lips close enough to send a chill down my neck. Then he kisses just beneath my ear, slow and lingering, like he's trying to remind me of every single thing I left behind.

"Symere."

"Hmm?"

"You tryna distract me."

He smiles against my skin. "I *am* the distraction, baby. Always been."

I laugh, but my stomach tightens. "So, you just out here seducing people in airport lots now?"

He grins. "Only the ones who I've been deep inside of, baby."

I nudge his chest gently. "Let me in the car before I embarrass myself."

He steps back just enough to open the passenger door, brushing my ass as I climb in. On purpose.

"You felt that?"

"You ain't slick."

He winks. "Ain't tryin' to be."

Once he's behind the wheel, he glances over at me like he's trying to read a story across my skin.

"You sure you ready?"

I nod. "I wouldn't be here if I wasn't."

"We didn't change," he says. "Still want you. Still gon' have you, if you let us. But only if you stay."

My hand finds his on the console. Fingers lacing.

"I came to find out what we could be. If it's still there."

He brings my hand to his mouth, kisses my knuckles. "It never left."

And just like that, the tension in my chest starts to unravel.

"Let's go home," I whisper.

"Say less."

The drive is smooth. Familiar streets blur past as Symere navigates through traffic with one hand on the wheel, the other resting on my thigh like it's always belonged there. His thumb moves in slow, lazy circles just above my knee, and the silence between us feels full instead of awkward. Every now and then, he glances over at me, eyes soft but focused, like he's still making sure I'm really here.

"You quiet," he says finally, voice low.

I shrug. "Just thinking."

"'Bout us?"

"Yeah."

His hand squeezes my thigh. "Good. We been thinking about you too."

The words hang between us, thick with promise.

By the time we pull into the driveway, my nerves are a tangled mess. I haven't seen Maleia since I left that morning, wrapped in one of her silk robes with my heart in pieces. We've texted, sure, but nothing close to the way it used to be. And now I'm about to walk back into their space, their life, their love, and hope there's still room for me.

Before I can overthink it, the front door swings open.

"Honesti! Happy Thanksgiving!"

Maleia's voice cuts through the quiet like sunshine, and then she's rushing down the steps barefoot, curls bouncing, sweater hanging off one shoulder, leggings hugging every curve. She looks radiant, like joy incarnate.

I barely get one foot out of the car before she's pulling me into a tight hug.

Her lips land on mine fast, soft, and sure. It's instinct more than anything, like muscle memory. I don't hesitate this time. I pull her in closer, wrap an arm around her waist, and kiss her back deep, purposeful. My other hand finds the side of her face, tilting her chin so I can take more. Let her feel everything I've kept bottled up for the last year.

She breathes out a soft sound against my mouth, like a gasp and a whimper all in one. Then she pulls back just enough to look at me.

"Oh my God," she whispers. "I shouldn't have—"

"Don't finish that," I cut in, brushing my thumb over her cheek. "You don't have to be sorry. I wanted that. Been wanting that."

Her fingers tighten at my waist. "You sure?"

"Yeah, I promise, baby girl."

Her smile blooms, slow and wide.

Symere's arms wrap around us both from behind, solid and sure. "Y'all good?"

Maleia leans into him but doesn't let go of me. Her fingers stay laced at my hip like she's not ready to give up the contact.

"Better than good," she says. "She came home."

He presses a kiss to her temple, then meets my gaze over her curls. "And she ain't runnin' this time."

I shake my head. "Not planning on it."

We stay locked together for a minute, wrapped up in each other like a knot that finally makes sense.

Then Maleia laughs and breaks the moment. "Come on inside before I start crying and the neighbors get something to talk about."

The house smells like vanilla and something savory in the oven. Warm, lived-in, familiar. Nothing's changed, but every-thing feels different. Or maybe that's just me.

Symere grabs my bag while Maleia leads me in by the hand, her thumb stroking across my knuckles.

"You hungry?" she asks.

"Starving."

"Good. I made that mac and cheese you love. And don't act brand new. You know how we do Friendsgiving."

I let her tug me deeper into the house, into their world. Into whatever we're about to become.

Because I'm not running anymore.

Not from them.

Not from this.

Not again.

———

The plates are cleared, the house still humming with warmth and wine and unspoken want. No one says what's thick in the air. We all feel it. It lingers in the corners of the room, rides the lull in conversation, and settles between shared glances and subtle touches.

After dinner, Maleia curls up next to me on the couch. Her thigh brushes mine, her hand resting on my leg like it belongs there. Symere moves around the kitchen, rinsing plates and stacking dishes, but his eyes keep cutting back to us. There's a twitch in his jaw, a glance too long to be casual.

"Y'all good?" he asks, drying his hands on a towel.

Maleia hums, soft and sweet. "Mmhmm."

He nods toward the hallway. "Let's call it. You had a long-ass flight, little rabbit. We'll catch up more tomorrow."

She rises first, and I follow. Maleia walks me to the guest room, flicks on the light and steps aside. The room smells like lavender and fresh linen. There's a folded blanket at the foot of the bed and a water bottle on the nightstand.

"You need anything?" she asks, still standing in the doorway.

I shake my head. "No. This is perfect."

She smiles, something lingering in her gaze before she quietly closes the door.

I undress slowly, the buzz from dinner still humming in my blood. Their energy never left me. It's wrapped around my skin like a second layer. I slide under the covers in a tank top and panties, turn toward the wall, and try to settle. But my body doesn't want to sleep. It wants more.

Fifteen minutes pass.

Then I hear it.

A deep grunt. A moan, low and breathy. Maleia. The bed creaks. The rhythm picks up quickly.

"You miss this dick, huh?" Symere's voice cuts through the thin walls, low and full of heat. "Couldn't even hide it at dinner."

She whines softly, her answer broken by the pace of his thrusts.

"You were lookin' at me like you needed this just to breathe."

Another moan. A cry, high-pitched and unfiltered.

The slap of skin meeting skin gets louder. He's not holding back. The force behind his movements rattles something in me. The sound of her gasps, her whimpers, they're real. Raw.

"You stay drippin' when I'm in you like this. Tight as hell, and all mine."

"Yours," she pants.

"You know what I think?" he says, voice rougher now. "I think you want her, too. Thinkin' about her when I'm deep in you like this. I saw the way you looked at her earlier. Bet your pussy got wetter just bein' near her."

She doesn't answer. Just another moan, longer this time.

He groans. "Yeah. That's what I thought. You want her to fuck you, huh? Want her to ride your face like she's starved. You want her deep inside you while I'm stretchin' you from the back."

Maleia cries out, her voice breaking like it's too much. Like it's everything.

My hand slips between my thighs, slick and ready. The way he's talking to her, about me, it pulls the need right out of me.

I rub slow, in sync with the rhythm of their bodies, the rise and fall of her moans.

"You greedy for it, Li," he murmurs. "You want her just as bad as I do. Don't gotta say it. I feel it in the way you're squeezin' me."

Another sharp cry. Another hard thrust. The bed slams the wall.

"Yeah," Symere growls. "Let it go. That's it, baby. Come for me."

She shatters on a moan that makes my hand move faster. My climax hits just as hers breaks through the air, like we're tied together in sound, in heat, in want.

I come with a gasp, trembling under the sheets, my skin flushed and tingling.

They don't know I can hear them.

They're not performing for me.

But it still pulls me deeper.

The house settles. The bed next door quiets. My breath slows, but the ache doesn't leave.

They're not waiting on me.

But they haven't let me go either.

Next time, I won't be behind this wall.

Next time, I'll be right where I belong, between them.

two

. . .

I Remember How You Taste

THE SMELL of bacon and rich coffee drifts up the stairs and tugs me from sleep. My eyes open slowly, the quiet hum of the house settling in before anything else. It's not just the scent that wakes me, but the low memory of the night before. Their voices. The way they said my name.

I stretch, muscles tight from sleep, heart still a little heavy from everything I've carried. I glance toward the space beside me. Empty.

I slip out of bed, brush my teeth, wash my face, and step into the shower. The hot water eases the tension from my body, helping to quiet the thoughts still racing from last night. Afterward, I towel off, unwrap my bonnet, and carefully smooth down my silk press. I study my reflection in the mirror. I look like me again. More than that, I look ready.

I take my time getting dressed. After smoothing down my hair, I reach for my favorite shea butter blend from Exclusive Botanical, Passion and Wedding Cake. The scent clings to my skin, warm and sweet like lemon-lavender pound cake. I slip into a cropped white tank that clings to my chest, no bra, letting the cool air kiss my skin. My shorts are black silk, skimming just below the curve of my ass. I want them to see me. To want me.

I pad downstairs quietly, the scent growing stronger as I near the kitchen. Laughter floats from around the corner. I pause at the edge of the room. Maleia and Symere are dancing, slow and easy, lost in their own little world. She's wrapped in his arms, her laughter spilling out as he dips her, playful and smooth. It knocks the air from my lungs, seeing how effortless they are together. How right they look.

That could've been mine, too.

I linger for a moment, fingers trailing along the wall, before I gather myself and step forward. The hardwood is cool beneath my feet as I enter the kitchen.

"Well damn," Symere says, dragging his gaze down slowly.

Maleia smiles, heat behind her eyes. "Good morning, pretty girl."

I walk over to them, stepping between their bodies and pressing a kiss to Maleia's lips, then Symere's. His hand curls around my waist, lips firm and hot. He catches my bottom lip for a second longer, like he wants more.

Before he can say anything else, his phone buzzes on the counter. He sighs and grabs it, glancing at the screen. "One of the trucks got held up at the site. If I don't fix it now, it'll throw off the whole pour."

Maleia rubs his chest gently. "You need us to come with you?"

He shakes his head. "Nah. Y'all stay. Eat, relax, shop if you want. Cards on the counter. I'll be back soon."

He grabs his thermos, kisses Maleia deeply, then kisses me again, tongue sweeping into my mouth. It's possessive and slow, like he's reminding me who I belong to. My knees go a little weak.

Then he's out the door, boots thudding against the porch.

Maleia turns back to the stove, flipping the last strips of bacon. Her eyes drift to mine. "You okay?"

I nod, brushing a loose curl behind my ear. "Yeah. Just... can we talk?"

She cuts the burner off and slides the pan aside. "Of course. Let's sit."

We move to the island, settling across from each other. The air is warm, humming with all the unspoken things we've been holding.

"I thought about you every day," I say, fingers tracing the rim of my mug. "Even when I was pretending I didn't."

She tilts her head, watching me. "Then why'd you run?"

My chest tightens. "Because it scared me. Wanting something that deep, that permanent. I didn't know how to want it without thinking I'd lose it."

Her expression doesn't shift, but there's something softer in her eyes. "You already had it, Honesti. You still do. But you didn't trust us enough to say it then."

I reach for her hand across the island. Our fingers touch, and the ache in my chest eases. "I trust you now. Both of you."

"We're not asking for forever all at once," she says, voice low. "Just don't disappear again."

"I won't," I promise.

She stands and gently pulls me to my feet. "Then come help me finish breakfast. After that, we make good use of Symere's card."

A smirk pulls at my lips. "You sure he can handle the damage?"

"Baby, that man builds mansions. He'll be just fine."

We move around the kitchen like we've done this a thousand times. Coffee is poured, plates filled, and laughter begins to bubble between us. The weight we've carried isn't gone, but it doesn't feel so heavy now.

When she brushes against me at the sink, her hand settling on the small of my back, I lean into it. The warmth spreads, quiet and full. For the first time in a long while, it doesn't feel like I'm chasing something. It feels like I've finally come home.

The sunlight filtered through the windshield as we pulled into the mall parking lot, that lazy kind of morning warmth softening everything. I had the music low, some old H-Town playing, the bass vibrating just enough to settle in our chests. Maleia hummed along from the passenger seat, her body angled toward me like she didn't have a care in the world.

Symere's black card was already tucked into her wallet.

"He's gonna regret giving us free rein like this," she said, stretching like a cat, her crop top lifting just enough to show a sliver of soft skin.

I smirked, cutting the engine. "He won't. He already knows what time it is."

She laughed, low and full of mischief. That sound had always done something to me. Still did.

Inside, the mall buzzed with holiday energy but not the overwhelming kind. We wandered with linked arms, stopping here and there to touch fabrics, smell candles, and play with makeup we didn't need. Maleia flirted with every sales rep who gave her attention. I stayed close, watching her soak it up, cataloging every sly smile and every extra sway of her hips.

I didn't make her carry any bags. That was my job today. She liked to touch things, and I liked watching her do it.

The shift happened subtly, like the weather changing. We passed a boutique with soft lighting and a muted blush color scheme. Satin and lace displays are draped like whispers in the window.

Maleia slowed, one hand brushing the edge of the door.

"You thinking what I'm thinking?" I asked, voice low.

She gave me a look over her shoulder, eyes glittering. "I'm always thinking worse."

We stepped inside.

The boutique smelled like vanilla and something faintly floral. A woman behind the counter greeted us, but we barely registered her. Maleia drifted toward a rack of lace bodysuits, her fingers dancing over the delicate material.

"Pick two," I said, stepping closer and whispering into her ear. "I'm gonna tear one off of you."

She raised a brow, a teasing smile creeping up. Without a word, she pulled down an olive green lace set and another in deep burgundy.

"You'd better come with me," she said, voice light but her eyes heavy.

The dressing room was small and dimly lit, mirror-lined and intimate. She didn't hesitate. Clothes slipped off with casual grace. I sat on the bench, watching every move, hunger curled low in my belly.

She stepped into the green set, the fabric hugging her like it was made for her. She turned slowly, letting me take it in.

"You good?" she asked, cocking her hip.

Instead of answering, I pulled out my phone and snapped a picture.

"Honesti," she gasped.

"Relax. Gotta make sure Symere sees what you're spending his money on."

I sent it to Symere.

Me:

> She out here acting up. Permission to handle it?

He replied quickly.

Symere:

> FaceTime me.

I hit the button and angled the phone toward the mirror. She met his gaze through the screen, steady, bold.

"Look at her," I said.

He exhaled. "Lord."

"You want her to behave?" I asked.

He smirked. "Nah. I want her to pay for teasing you."

I turned to her.

"Mirror. Hands up."

She obeyed, slow and deliberate.

My palm landed on the curve of her ass, sharp and echoing.

"One."

She tensed, lips parted. I glanced at the screen. Symere's eyes were locked on her.

Another slap, then another. I didn't count out loud after that. I just watched the way her thighs flexed, how she rocked onto the balls of her feet, breath catching each time.

"All that touching, all that looking at me wanted me to do this. I didn't get to play with you much last year. I think you forgot how good I ate that pretty, little pussy. " I murmured in her ear.

"I didn't forget," she said, voice barely there.

I slid my hand down, moving the lace aside. She was soaked.

Symere groaned through the phone. "Make her cum, little rabbit."

I slipped two fingers inside her. Slow. Measured. Just enough.

She gasped, gripping the mirror harder.

"You better keep quiet," I warned. "Ain't nobody supposed to know what we doing."

She nodded, biting her lip. Her body rocked back onto my hand, needy.

I pulled out.

She whined, frustrated.

"You think you run this? You think teasing me gets you what you want?"

"I was just playing," she said.

"Play again and see what happens."

I pushed back in, curling my fingers just right. Her knees buckled slightly.

"You close?"

She nodded, face buried in her arm.

I stopped again.

"Ask nice."

She looked at the screen. Symere stared back, eyes dark.

"Please. I need it. I'll be good."

He nodded slowly. "Let her."

This time, I didn't hold back. My hand moved faster, deeper, the pressure just enough to drag her over the edge. Her moan was low and broken, her legs trembling.

I held her through it, fingers stilling only when her breath steadied.

When I finally helped her back into her clothes, we didn't speak. We didn't need to.

We paid for both body suits, and the cashier smirked at us, knowingly, and told us to have a good rest of our day.

Outside the boutique, she slid her hand into mine. Our fingers laced together.

And I knew we weren't pretending anymore. I'm right where I was meant to be.

————

We made it back to the house still buzzing from the day, the kind of tired that was more about satisfaction than exhaustion. The door closed behind us with a soft click, the weight of shopping bags left in a neat heap by the front closet. Laughter lingered, sticky-sweet and low, as we moved through the space like we belonged in it.

"Movie while we wait on him?" Maleia asked, glancing at me over her shoulder. Her voice carried a hint of suggestion, subtle but unmistakable.

I gave her a nod, the corner of my mouth lifting. "Yeah. Let's pick something dumb we won't actually finish."

She smirked and headed for the stairs. "I'm changing into something cozy."

I watched her go, then turned toward the kitchen. The fridge opened with a hum, and I grabbed a few drinks, some kettle corn, and a half-eaten container of cookie dough. No need to pretend we were watching for the plot.

Back in my room, I peeled off my bralette and shorts, trading them for a pair of soft cotton boyshorts and an oversized, cropped tee. It hugged my waist and hinted at everything underneath. Just enough. I tossed my hair up in a loose bun and padded back downstairs.

Maleia was already on the couch, curled into the corner like she'd been waiting for me her whole life. She wore a long-sleeve, cropped shirt that clung to her chest and matching shorts so short they were practically underwear. Her legs were bare and stretched out, smooth and glowing.

She tilted her head as I set the snacks down. "Look at you. All that cake and no celebration."

I laughed, flopping down beside her. "Keep talking like that and you'll get a mouthful."

She grinned and leaned in. "That's the plan."

We queued up a movie, something with a ridiculous plot and a pretty cast, just enough background noise to pretend. Her thigh brushed against mine. I leaned back, stretching out while sipping soda, pretending not to notice her hand inching over.

Ten minutes in, she leaned into my ear. "I've been thinking about your taste since the dressing room."

My head turned slowly. "You want something, Li?"

Her eyes flickered down to my thighs. "I wanna eat your pussy ."

I stared at her, heartbeat thudding low and slow. "Show me then."

She didn't waste a second. Her hands slipped under the hem of my shirt, fingertips skating along my stomach. She eased my boy shorts down, eyes locked on mine as she helped me out of them completely.

I leaned back on the couch, legs open just enough to invite her. She dropped to her knees on the rug in front of me, licking her lips.

"Look at you," she murmured. "Already wet for me. I wanna make you cum in my mouth."

I raised an eyebrow. "Earn it, pretty girl."

And she did. Her mouth was hot, tongue tracing the seam of my folds before she latched onto my clit like she'd missed it. My head tipped back, breath catching in my throat.

"Mmm, yeah... just like that," I moaned. "You're eating my pussy so good, like you're trying to convince me to stay."

She moaned into me, and the vibration sent a jolt through my spine. I threaded my fingers into her curls, guiding her, keeping her right where I wanted.

"Such a good girl," I breathed. "You love it when I talk to you like this, don't you? You love knowing that you're eating my pussy so good."

She nodded against me, the movement making my thighs tighten. I rocked into her face, grinding gently as her tongue flicked and curled with practiced control. The first orgasm hit hard. My legs trembled, breath coming in stuttered gasps as I cried out.

She didn't stop, didn't even slow. My hips twitched from the sensitivity, but she drank it in like she was starving.

I tugged her up, pulling her into my lap. She kissed me messy and open-mouthed, tongue still tasting of me.

"Lie back," I commanded, voice hoarse. "Now."

Maleia laid across the cushions, hair sprawled like a halo. I climbed over her, tugging her shorts down her legs and tossing them somewhere behind us. Her pussy was already glistening, lips swollen.

I didn't tease. My mouth was on her immediately, tongue flattening and sliding up her center.

"Fuck!" she gasped, hips bucking into me.

I moaned into her, loving how reactive she was. I licked her slowly at first, then sucked her clit with a rhythm that had her fingers digging into the couch.

"That's it," I cooed. "You taste so fucking good, baby. So wet for me."

Her legs quivered, cries breaking free. I slid two fingers inside her, curling up to find that spot that made her come undone.

"You wanna cum again for me?" I asked.

"Yes..please, Honesti. I need it."

I kissed her inner thigh. "Then give it to me."

She came with a scream, hips grinding wildly as I held her down. Her body went limp, chest rising and falling fast. I crawled up and kissed her, biting her bottom lip before pulling back.

"Flip over."

She obeyed. I straddled her chest, lowering myself onto her mouth. Her tongue met me eagerly, lapping at me while I moaned and rocked.

I leaned down, sucking her clit as her moans vibrated through me. We fed on each other, desperate and wild. It wasn't graceful. It was raw, messy, and perfect.

My second orgasm came as hers hit again, our bodies jerking together, legs locked. I collapsed onto her, both of us breathless.

I pushed her gently onto her back, our lips brushing. "One more."

She nodded, eyes heavy. I lined our hips and began to grind, the friction hot and immediate.

Our slick pussies rubbed together, clits kissing, bodies rolling in sync. I cupped her breasts, rolling her nipples between my fingers as I whispered against her mouth.

"Your pussy feels so good rubbing on mine. I could've been fucking you like this for so long."

She cried out, body arching. I picked up the pace, our moans tangling as we chased the high.

When we came together, it was blinding. My thighs trembled, her nails scratched down my back, and the room spun for a second.

Just as the echoes faded, the front door opened.

Boots. Keys.

We froze.

Symere's voice rolled through the space. "Y'all really couldn't wait for me, huh?"

His footsteps neared, and I didn't even bother to move. I looked over my shoulder, still straddling Maleia, lips parted and skin flushed.

"Told you we were trouble."

three

. . .

Say Ours Mine and Mean It

THE SOUND of my boots tapping against the hardwood echoed through the house. It was the only thing speaking in that moment, louder than the breath still heavy in the air, louder than the creak of the mattress upstairs. I didn't rush. I didn't ask questions. Their bodies told me everything before I even reached the top of the stairs.

Skin flushed. Thighs slick. Legs tangled like they'd been trying to become one. The kind of aftermath that didn't lie.

But what really set me off was the way they looked at me when I stepped into that doorway. Innocent. Like they ain't just made each other scream loud enough to rattle the walls. Like they forgot whose house this was. Whose name sat on that deed.

I didn't smile. Didn't blink.

"Upstairs. Now."

No hesitation. Honesti moved first. She walked like a woman who knew she was in trouble but welcomed it. Defiant, steady, chin up like she wore the punishment like a crown. Maleia followed behind, legs a little wobbly, lips red and swollen, face flushed like she'd just been wrecked. I waited until the bedroom door clicked shut before heading into the bathroom.

Quick rinse. Fast enough to scrub off the grit of the job site, slow enough to calm the blaze starting in my chest. The water pelted against my shoulders, and still I couldn't cool off. Not with the image of their tangled bodies fresh in my mind. Not with my dick already thick and heavy, aching to claim what was mine.

When I stepped into the bedroom, towel slung low on my hips, they were both on the bed waiting.

Maleia lying on her back, hair spread across the pillow like silk, her body relaxed and legs parted, offering herself up without shame. Honesti sat beside her, hand lazily tracing the curve of Maleia's waist, her gaze cutting sharp to me the second I walked in.

"Honesti. Straddle her face."

Honesti didn't miss a beat. She moved with a steady, sultry grace, easing forward until her knees framed Maleia's flushed cheeks. With one hand, she spread herself open, and Maleia dove in without hesitation, tongue flicking with purpose, like she had something to prove and a point to make.

"She loves the taste of you, little rabbit." I asked, voice low and rough. "Now get my dick ready for her so I can fuck her tight pussy."

Honesti stayed straddling Maleia's face, hips rolling with slow control as her eyes locked onto mine. She didn't move to get off until I gave a slight nod. Only then did she ease off, slick and breathless, crawling toward me with heat still in her eyes. Her fingers tugged the towel loose from my hips, letting it drop. She gripped me firmly, delivering slow strokes full of intent, as if she were memorizing every vein and weight. Her lips followed, warm and slick, tongue tracing along the length before she swallowed me inch by inch, her gaze never breaking from mine.

"Make it nasty."

She did. Spit bubbled at the corners of her mouth, dripping down her chin in thick ropes. Her hand twisted in sync with every wet slurp, her lips stretching wide to take me deeper, throat flexing as she swallowed around me. She pulled back and sucked on that vein under my dick like it pulsed just for her. Loud, nasty, eyes blazing like she loved being watched. I groaned, the sound guttural, my hand clenching the back of her neck as she drove herself harder, turning my knees to jelly with every drag of her mouth.

I pulled away before I lost it, breathing hard. "Ride her face."

She obeyed, sliding her hands along Maleia's chest, fingers pinching and tugging her nipples just enough to make her squirm. I turned to Maleia, coaxing her hips to the edge of the bed, then pulled her leg over my thigh until she was open and ready for me. Her pussy shimmered, slick and needy, her inner thighs trembling from the orgasm Honesti delivered her while I was gone. I knelt down, kissed along her calf, letting my lips drag slow and warm over her skin before gripping her thighs. I slid her thigh over my shoulder before sliding into her in one deep, deliberate thrust that stretched her around me, burying myself until there was nowhere else to go.

She gasped, arching beneath me.

"Take this dick, baby. Feel me up all in yo guts." I rumbled, leaning over her with a slow grind that dragged a moan from her throat. "You feel how deep I am in that pussy? Now don't stop eatin' her pussy because if you do, I'm gonna stop fuckin' you ."

Maleia didn't stop. Her mouth was already back on Honesti, licking and sucking like she was starving. I watched the way Honesti melted under her, the way her body bucked every time Maleia's tongue hit just right.

"Rub her clit slow and mean," I growled. "Work her just right till she squirts all over us. I wanna feel that mess drip down my dick while I'm buried in her."

Honesti moaned and reached down, rubbing small, tight circles against Maleia's clit. I grabbed Maleia's hips tighter and started fucking into her harder, the wet sound of skin meeting skin echoing around the room.

"That's it," I grunted. "She's losing it for you. You feel that? She's about soaking the both of us."

Maleia cried out, her pussy tightening as she came again, back arching off the bed. I didn't stop, grinding into her until she sagged beneath me.

Then I reached for Honesti, dragging her off Maleia and into my lap. Her back to my chest, I pulled her thighs wide, my hand circling her throat as I kissed along her shoulder. My other hand found her pussy and I rubbed her slow, teasing her until she trembled.

I shifted, angling her over my knee, lining up and sliding into her from behind, slow and deep, filling her inch by inch.

"Yeah," I breathed against her neck. "That's it. Take all this dick. You mine now. Ours. No more runnin', little rabbit."

She cried out, body rocking against me as I held her in place, my hand on her neck, my lips pressed to her jaw.

"You feel that? That's me stretchin' you open so you don't forget."

I fucked into her with deep strokes, slow and possessive, until she was gasping. I held her tight, filling her up until my release hit, spilling into her with a groan. I stayed there, buried inside, letting her feel every bit of it.

She was ours now. All of her.

———

The steam from the shower curled around us like a warm fog, softening everything in its path. Water drummed steadily against our skin, washing away sweat, salt, and the lingering scent of what we'd just done. Maleia stood behind Honesti, arms wrapped loosely around her waist, head tucked against her shoulder. I stood facing them, rinsing the soap from my chest, letting the moment slow.

No one spoke at first. We didn't have to. Our bodies communicated in the way they leaned into one another, in the silent exchanges of fingertips brushing skin, in the quiet knowing that lingers after you've shed more than just fabric. The kind of closeness that speaks louder than words ever could.

Honesti's lashes were damp, her skin flushed from both the heat and everything that had come before. She leaned back into Maleia's hold with a comfort that hadn't existed just days ago. Seeing it, feeling it, the weight in my chest pressed down and lifted all at once.

When the water started to cool, we stepped out one by one, drying off in silence. I passed Honesti a towel, watching the way her hands moved across her body, slow and unhurried. Like she was learning herself all over again.

We moved to the bedroom without needing to say a word. Maleia tugged one of my shirts over her head and slid under the covers. Honesti followed, slipping into a soft tank and panties before curling beside her. I joined them last, easing between them, one arm draped over each waist. The room dimmed to a quiet hush, the air still warm with what lingered.

It was Honesti who broke the silence first. Her voice was quiet but full of something that clutched deep.

"How are we doing this?"

I turned my head toward her. "What you mean, baby?"

She looked up at the ceiling like she could piece the answer together if she stared long enough. "Us. This. I don't want it to be just a moment we look back on. I want it to be something we build."

Maleia slid her hand along Honesti's thigh, grounding her. "We want that too. You're not alone in this."

"I had a whole life in Houston," she said softly. "Clients. A house. My studio."

I sat up slightly, resting on one elbow so I could see her fully. "You thinkin' about givin' it all up?"

She looked at me, her expression already telling the truth. "I already did."

My breath caught. "Say that again."

Her voice trembled just enough to hit me square in the chest. "I sold my house. Closed my studio. I made peace with walking away before I even got in the car to come here. I just needed to know if this was real before I said it out loud."

Maleia's eyes welled, her hand covering her mouth. I reached for Honesti's hand and pulled it to my chest, where my heart thudded steady.

"You let go of everything just to be with us?"

She nodded. "It didn't feel like losing anything. It felt like making room. Like clearing space for something that's mine. For something I want."

That undid me a little. Not in a dramatic way, but in a quiet, soul-deep kind of way. I didn't speak right away. Just held her hand tighter, let the weight of her decision settle over me.

"You got a home here. Not just a place to stay. A home."

Maleia leaned in, tears slipping free. She cupped Honesti's cheek, brushing her thumb along the bone. "We'll figure it out. All of it. The little things, the big things. We'll make it work. Together."

Honesti blinked up at us, voice barely above a whisper. "I want it to work. But I'm scared. What if I mess this up? What if it's too much?"

I slid my arm under her head, pulling her closer. "Then we talk. We listen. We fight fair. But we don't walk away, not unless we're walkin' toward each other."

Maleia nodded. "You're not just some addition to what we already have. You're part of it now. You are family. We've been missing a piece, and it's always been you."

Honesti's tears came in quiet waves. She didn't fight them. She didn't try to cover her face or pretend they weren't there. She let them fall, let herself be seen in the rawest way.

"I thought I was being reckless," she said, her voice cracking. "I kept telling myself it was too soon, too risky. But the truth is, I've never been more certain about anything. I don't want to be anywhere else."

"You don't have to have it all figured out," I told her. "We'll hold you down while you find your rhythm again. You got space to breathe here. To create again when you're ready."

Maleia rested her forehead against Honesti's, brushing her nose gently. "Let this be your soft place to land. Let us be that."

Honesti reached for both of our hands, threading her fingers with ours. "Thank you. For not asking me to choose. For being patient when I wasn't sure how to stay."

I kissed the back of her hand, then leaned in to kiss her forehead. "You're ours now. You showed up for us, and we gon' keep showin' up for you."

"Every day," Maleia whispered. "As long as you let us."

We didn't talk after that. Not for a long while. We just laid there in the dim glow of the room, wrapped around each other like the answer to a question none of us could name. And maybe that was the most honest part of it all—we didn't need perfect words or flawless plans. We just needed this. Each other. And the willingness to stay.

four

· · ·

If You Can't Respect Us, Don't Sit Here

THE HOUSE BRIMMED with warmth and noise, the kind of joyful chaos that came with too many bodies and not enough chairs. Golden Saturday sunlight filtered through the wide dining room windows, dancing off glasses and silverware. Every surface groaned under the weight of food, from candied yams and roasted turkey to greens cooked just right and dressing so rich it barely needed gravy. The scent of sage, honey, and something sweet like cinnamon clung to the air.

We had opened our home for Thanksgiving, both families packed in like we were already one. Cousins traded jokes and memories, uncles laughed too loud at the game in the next room, and aunties compared notes on whose pie was the flakiest. It was the kind of gathering I used to dream about when I was little, full of love, noise, and comfort. But this one had my name on it. Ours.

Honesti looked beautiful tonight. She wore a wine-colored wrap dress that hugged her just right, curls bouncing with each step. She moved through the crowd like she belonged in it, smiling, helping where she could, listening with her whole body. I watched her from across the room, and my heart twisted. She had given up everything in Houston to be here. To be with us. This holiday was supposed to be proof that she was already home.

"Maleia, this dressing hittin'," my cousin Zaire said, scooping another helping onto his plate.

I laughed, bumping his shoulder. "Told you. That's Honesti's recipe. She hooked it up."

"Oh, so she cookin' now too?" one of my aunts joked, smiling across the table.

Honesti grinned modestly. "Just trying to hold my own."

The house felt full in every way. It was Saturday, crisp and cool outside, but inside, warmth wrapped around us like a blanket. Sunlight poured in and bathed the dining room in a soft golden glow. The table Symere built stretched across the room, holding plates of cornbread dressing, glazed ham, roasted sweet potatoes, and thick, cheesy macaroni. Wine glasses clinked, kids ran back and forth past the grown folks, and the hum of conversations floated over it all.

We sat beside each other once the food was served. My leg brushed hers under the table, a quiet reminder that she was mine. Across from us, Symere was telling a story that had my uncle wheezing from laughter. For a while, it felt easy. Like everything had fallen into place.

Until my mama opened her mouth.

She set her fork down and looked across the table at Honesti, like she'd been waiting for the right moment to start something. "So, what exactly do you do with yourself again?"

Honesti's smile didn't falter. "I'm a photographer. I do portraits, editorial work, and brand campaigns."

"Huh," Mama said, taking a slow sip from her wine glass. "And that pays bills?"

The room quieted. Conversations slowed. Even the football game in the next room felt muted.

Honesti stayed calm. "It does. I've been doing it full-time for years."

"Interesting," Mama said. "I guess some people can get by chasing dreams. Good thing Symere's got real money. Supporting two women though? That's something else."

My jaw clenched. "Mama, we not doing that today."

She held up a hand like she was being reasonable. "Don't get your panties in a bunch, Maleia. I'm just saying what everybody's thinking. This little setup y'all got going? Folks might smile, but behind closed doors, they shaking their heads."

Zaire cleared his throat, shifting uncomfortably. My aunt stared down at her plate. Honesti kept her eyes on her lap.

"And I didn't know we letting side bitches eat with the family now," Mama added with a smirk. "But I guess this new generation really don't care about appearances."

The air was sucked from the room. No clinks, no chewing, no chatter. Just silence thick enough to drown in.

Honesti rose slowly. She didn't raise her voice, didn't make a scene. She just stood, picked up her napkin, and walked out of the room with her head held high.

Mama let out a sharp laugh like she'd made a point. "See? That right there. Sensitive. If she can't take a little truth, she ain't built for this."

I wanted to follow her so bad, to wrap my arms around her and block out every nasty thing that had just happened. But I stayed rooted in place, knowing Symere was already gonna handle it.

Symere's fork hit the plate with a sharp clink, louder than the silence Mama's words left behind. He sat still for a breath, then another, his jaw flexing as he scanned the table. No one would meet his gaze. Not a cousin, not an auntie, not even Zaire, who'd been cracking jokes minutes earlier. All of them suddenly quiet. All of them complicit.

He stood slowly, chair legs dragging across the floor. He didn't yell. Just set both hands on the table, fingers spread wide like he was anchoring himself there. His voice came low, cool, the kind of calm that made your chest tighten.

"Let me make somethin' real clear."

Heads turned. The air stiffened.

"Y'all don't ever get to disrespect my woman in my house. I don't care what you think you know or how you feel about it. You come at her, you comin' at me. And that's a problem you don't want."

His voice picked up steam, deeper now, rougher. "Y'all love pretendin' like you got morals, like you ain't done dirt, like you're better than us. But some of y'all ain't got a damn leg to stand on. Don't sit here with food in your mouth and judgment in your heart."

Mama opened her mouth to speak. Symere didn't let her. He cut a look her way so sharp it might as well have slapped her.

"Don't. Unless you got an apology ready. And it better be sincere. Otherwise, keep that mess to yourself."

Zaire looked away, ashamed. One of the aunties fidgeted with her napkin but didn't speak.

I pushed my chair back with a screech. My voice rang clear. "Let's not pretend y'all saints. Aunt Carol, your husband got a baby with his own cousin, and you actin' like I'm the embarrassment? Please."

I turned to Uncle Keith. "Still behind on child support but showin' up here like you father of the year."

Then Cousin Tasha, who had the nerve to whisper under her breath earlier. "You out here judging me when your last girlfriend had to take out a restraining order. Sit down."

I took a breath and looked around the table. "Keep Honesti's name out your mouths. That woman gave up everything— her business, her city, her whole life—for us. She didn't come here to be tolerated. She came here to be loved. And if you can't give her that, then you got no place at this table."

Symere stepped back in, voice smoother now but still strong. "Ain't nobody here begging y'all to understand. But if you can't show respect, get out."

Chairs scraped. Plates were pushed away. A few folks mumbled something like goodbyes, but most just filed out without a word. The front door closed one last time, and the silence left behind was thick, but clean.

"I'm going to her," I said, already on my feet.

I found Honesti in the guest room, sitting stiffly at the edge of the bed, her back to the door. Her arms were wrapped around herself like she was holding something broken together. Her dress, the one she picked out so carefully, now looked too heavy for her.

I walked over and slipped my arms around her from behind. I rested my chin on her shoulder.

"You didn't deserve that. None of it."

She shook her head. "I should've seen it coming."

"You shouldn't have had to," I said, turning her to face me. "That hate? That ain't on you. That's on them."

Her eyes met mine, glossy and red, then the tears fell. Quiet, like everything inside her had been stretched too thin.

Symere appeared in the doorway, then crossed the room and crouched in front of us. He took one of her hands, then mine.

"They're gone. And they ain't coming back unless you say so."

Honesti exhaled slowly. "I'm not leaving. I came here to stay. I want this. I want both of you."

My throat caught, but I smiled. "Then you got us. All of us. Every part. This is your home."

Symere reached up, resting a hand against the side of her face. "You ain't no guest. You not some side piece. You family. Our family. Period."

She nodded, lips trembling. "I'm yours. I've been yours."

The three of us leaned in, foreheads pressed together, hearts beating close.

———

It had been hours since the last guest left. The house was finally still, hushed and warm under the low lighting of the bedroom. The quiet was thick, but it wasn't empty. It was the kind that came after the storm, after hard truths were laid bare and the mess swept clean. The three of us had showered again, steam washing away more than just the day's grime. Now we were curled up in bed, limbs tangled, skin soft and smelling like lavender and something deeper, something ours.

I laid in the middle, Symere at my back, his arm slung over my waist, and Honesti in front of me, her head tucked beneath my chin. Her hand rested on my thigh, drawing slow, lazy circles that had nothing to do with sleep. My body hummed, still buzzing with everything we'd felt today. Everything we'd said.

Symere's voice broke the silence, low and rough like gravel and honey. "Y'all thought I forgot?"

Honesti shifted, lifting her head. "Forgot what?"

He smirked against my shoulder. "Said I was gonna reward y'all, remember? For being so damn good at the lingerie store."

My body reacted before my brain caught up, warmth blooming between my legs. I looked at Honesti, who smiled slowly, that smile that always made my stomach flip.

Symere sat up, back against the headboard, legs spread. "Come here. Both of you."

We crawled into position, Honesti on her knees beside me. He cupped her jaw. "What you want, baby?"

Her voice was soft, but sure. "I want your mouth on me while Maleia sucks your dick."

Symere groaned. "You nasty, and I love it."

He turned to me. "And you, Mrs. Owens?"

I bit my lip, heat rising. "I want you to fuck my pussy while Honesti straps up and takes my ass. I want y'all to fill me up together."

His eyes darkened. "Say less."

Symere leaned back against the pillows, motioning Honesti to straddle his face. She climbed over him, confident and hungry, knees firm on either side of his head. She hiked her dress up and peeled off her panties before lowering herself onto his mouth. A soft cry escaped her lips as his tongue met her heat.

I knelt between his legs, watching the way Honesti rolled her hips, trembling already. I reached for his dick, already hard and slick with anticipation. I licked the tip and took him into my mouth, slow and deep. His groan vibrated through Honesti, making her whimper and grip the headboard.

We moved together, me sucking him while she rode his face. Honesti leaned down, brushing her lips against mine before we passed his dick between us. We licked, sucked, and slurped, our spit glistening across his shaft. I kissed the thick vein underneath while she circled his tip with her tongue, slow and messy.

Symere pulled back just long enough to growl, "Maleia, come sit on it, baby. Time for your reward. You did so good bein' a pretty, little slut for Honesti."

Honesti climbed off him, headed to the drawer, and returned with the strap and lube. She handed him the bottle before fastening the harness onto her hips, tightening it with practiced ease.

I straddled his waist, knees pressed into the mattress. He pulled me down for a kiss, I could taste Honesti on his lips. Then he slid into me slowly, stretching me open until he was buried deep.

"Fuck," I gasped, head falling back.

Honesti slicked the strap on, watching us as Symere pumped into me with deep, rolling thrusts. He popped open the lube and poured some onto his fingers before circling my ass. Slow at first. Then one finger pushed in, two, twisting gently to open me up.

"She's ready," he said, voice thick.

Honesti stepped forward, the strap secured in place, slick and gleaming. She kissed the back of my neck, then lined herself up.

"Take a deep breath for me," she whispered, pressing in slowly.

The stretch was intense, both of them filling me inch by inch. I gasped, clutching at Symere's chest, forehead pressed to his as they rocked into me together.

"You feel us, baby ?" Symere groaned. "You feel how deep we are?"

"Yes," I choked, tears spilling from the corners of my eyes. "Oh my God, yes."

Honesti leaned over me, her body flush against mine, her hand gripping my waist. She moved in sync with Symere, their rhythm brutal and precise.

"Look at you," she whispered, her voice all reverence. "Taking both of us like the good girl you are. Our perfect, greedy girl."

I sobbed, lost in the heat, the stretch, the overwhelming love in every thrust and word. My body was trembling, sweat beading down my back. Every nerve ending felt raw.

They didn't stop. Didn't rush. Just gave and gave until I shattered, crying out their names, body wracked with wave after wave of pleasure.

When I came, it felt like flying apart, like breaking open in the best way. Symere was still inside me, thick and pulsing, his breath ragged. Honesti held me up, whispering sweet nothings into my ear.

And when the shaking stopped, and the silence returned,

they wrapped themselves around me. I realized this is how we should've been this entire time.

epilogue

. . .

Table For Three

THE SCENT of smoked turkey and sweet yams wrapped the house in warmth, the kind of warmth that seeped into your bones and reminded you that you were home. Laughter floated through each room, mingling with the crackle of old vinyl spinning slow jams and the bubbling sounds of pots on the stove. Heels clicked against the hardwood while voices layered into a rhythm only Black families could make—a harmony of jokes, gossip, and love. Sweet potato pie cooled beside peach cobbler, cinnamon, and brown sugar thick in the air like a second skin.

This wasn't just Thanksgiving. This was ours. Our home, our people, our love. A celebration built on hard conversations, louder laughs, and years of choosing each other on purpose.

The house stood just outside Atlanta, sitting bold on a stretch of land with red clay roots and Southern soul. It was all clean lines and warm brick, a wraparound porch made for sunrise coffee and late-night heart-to-hearts. Tall windows flooded each room with light. The backyard stretched wide enough to hold summer cookouts, bounce houses, and the soft pitter-patter of the babies we hadn't met yet. Symere built it with his own hands. Every beam carried a prayer. Every nail whispered intention.

He didn't build it for him and Maleia. He built it for us. From the dirt up, it belonged to all three of us.

A year had passed since we stood barefoot in that backyard, beneath Georgia skies, in front of everyone we loved. We tied ourselves together—not with tradition but with truth. Our bond ceremony was simple and sacred. Matching gold rings, each engraved with our date and a promise: *Ours. Always.* No more stacked bands. No reminders of before. Just one love, one choice, one future.

Our rhythms had settled. Some days came easily. Others came sharp-edged and sore. But every day, we moved as one. Even when we argued, we circled back to softness.

From the upstairs window, I watched cars fill the driveway. Family spilled out, arms full of food, voices raised in laughter. Somebody had already cranked up Frankie Beverly. Kids dashed across the lawn, high on sugar and cousins.

I rested my hand on the curve just starting beneath my sweater. Barely there to anyone else, but to me, it pulsed with everything I was becoming. Everything we were building.

I didn't hear her—never did—but I felt her. That quiet gravity that was uniquely Maleia.

She slipped beside me, linking her fingers with mine, resting her head on my shoulder.

"Symere's already circling them pies like he forgot how last year went," she said, her voice warm and velvet smooth.

I smirked. "He even *thinks* about that corner slice of sweet potato; he'll be sleeping on the porch tonight."

She laughed, a soft breath that brushed against my collarbone. Her other hand drifted to her own stomach, still flat. For now. We'd taken the tests together. Laughed. Cried. Swore ourselves to secrecy. Just for a while longer. Just ours.

"He gon' lose it," she murmured.

"Straight into the macaroni," I whispered back.

We giggled like we were seventeen again, not grown-ass women with jobs, rings, and babies on the way. But that was the thing about love—it kept the girl in you alive, even when the woman had bills and boundaries.

Downstairs, the house buzzed with joy. My photography studio had found its rhythm. What started as word of mouth blossomed into booked months, brand collabs, and mentorships for young Black girls with vision. My camera wasn't just my lens—it was my protest, my praise, my offering.

Maleia was walking fully in her calling now. She'd opened a child therapy center with rooms for music, painting, dance— all the ways children tell the truth when words fail them. She came home smelling like paint and purpose, stories sitting on the tip of her tongue, pride blooming in her chest.

Symere's construction business was thriving. He didn't chase skyscrapers. He rebuilt homes in neighborhoods people had given up on. Mentored boys who reminded him of his younger self—sharp-tongued, soft-hearted, needing a man to show them how to stay grounded without shrinking.

We weren't perfect. But we were thriving. Together.

Even when it meant making hard choices.

After last Thanksgiving, Maleia cut ties with her mama. Not out of anger, but protection. Some apologies came. Some didn't. But we didn't chase healing that refused to meet us halfway. We loved those who showed up with intention. That was enough.

We headed downstairs. The smell of collards and candied yams wrapped around us like a hug. Kids ran wild. Aunties clutched red cups and sharp side-eyes. Uncles shouted over the TV. And the playlist? Pure nostalgia.

Symere hovered too close to the dessert table.

"Boy, don't test me," I called out.

He turned, eyes wide with mock innocence. "I was just lookin'."

"Look from over there," Maleia added, arms crossed.

He strolled over, wrapped his arms around us, and kissed both our temples. "Y'all gon' bully me in my own house? That's crazy."

The dining table stretched long and rich. Dressed in greens, golden mac and cheese, cornbread dressing, fried chicken, glazed ham, and all the pies worth fighting over. Sweet potato, pecan, chess, and key lime.

We said grace. Plates passed. Laughter echoed like music. And somewhere between second helpings and stories about childhood fights, Maleia slipped her hand into mine.

"We did this," she whispered.

"All three of us," I replied, eyes on Symere across the table.

He didn't know yet. But he would. Soon.

We lingered around the table, bellies full and hearts wide open. The kind of full that only comes from food passed hand to hand, from collards that simmered all day, yams drenched in brown sugar, and laughter thick enough to season every bite. Kids darted between legs, snagging extra slices of pie and sneaking sips of red punch. Somebody's uncle was passed out in the recliner, mouth open, plate balanced on his chest like a badge of honor.

The whole house hummed with that Southern Black Thanksgiving energy. Old-school R&B crooned from the speakers, aunties laughed loud in the kitchen, and uncles yelled at the TV like their lives depended on the game. It was joy wrapped in tradition, layered with love and legacy.

Symere stood at the head of the table, hand resting on the back of his chair. The chatter dulled when he tapped his glass with a fork. That soft chime cut through the noise and brought everyone to stillness, like they could feel something was about to be said that mattered.

He took a breath. Looked out at everyone, but his eyes kept coming back to us.

"Y'all know I ain't big on speeches," he began, voice low and gravel-warm. "But tonight, I gotta speak from the heart."

A few folks chuckled, but most leaned in.

He turned first to Maleia. "You been my backbone since we were kids. My peace, my partner, my voice of reason, and my favorite kind of trouble. Through everything, you stayed. You grew with me. And I love you deeper than I got words for."

Then he turned to me, locking eyes like he saw every piece of me. "And you, Honesti. You didn't just come back into our lives. You anchored it. You didn't tiptoe around us or wait for permission. You stepped in with love, with grace, and never once made it feel like I had to split myself. You didn't fit in. You completed it."

My throat tightened. Maleia reached under the table and laced our fingers together.

He raised his glass. "To my girls. My two heartbeats. Who made this house feel like more than a place to live. Who made it home. To love that holds you up, pulls you close, and never lets you go."

The table erupted into cheers and glass clinks. My Uncle Rasco shouted, "Man, now I'm cryin' again!" and everyone cracked up.

Zaire leaned back in his chair, wiping his eyes with a napkin. "Boy, you done gone soft on us. We ain't never lettin' you live this down."

Maleia stood, pulling me up beside her. She held my hand like it was second nature.

"I'm thankful for a man who lets me be all of me. Who protects and provides, not just with his hands but with his heart. And for you, Honesti," she turned to me, smiling. "You didn't just walk back into our lives. You brought the missing piece. We're stronger because of you. Whole because you came back."

She turned back to Symere. "You held space for both of us. Loved us loud, loved us right. Thank you for being the kind of man that makes this love feel safe and sacred."

I swallowed hard, heart thudding. "I'm thankful for second chances. For choosing each other again and again. For the nights we talked until the sun rose, the days we fought and still held on. I'm thankful that you both didn't just open your home, you opened your hearts. You made room for me. And never once made me feel like a guest."

The murmurs circled the room. Napkins dabbed eyes. Aunt Vernetta nodded slowly, whispering, "That's real love."

Symere raised a brow, arms crossed. "That all, or y'all holdin' somethin' back?"

Maleia glanced at me, eyes shining.

"Actually," she said, lips curving into a slow smile, "we got one more thing."

I placed my hand gently on the small curve of my belly. "We both do."

A beat of silence passed. Then gasps hit the air like fireworks.

Symere blinked. "Wait... both?"

Maleia nodded, her grin wide now. "Yup. Took the tests together. Been keeping it on the low so we could tell you like this."

His mouth opened. Closed. Opened again. "You mean to tell me y'all both pregnant... and I ain't know a damn thing?"

Zaire shouted, "Boy, your swimmers got GPS!"

The whole table lost it. Symere barked out a laugh, pulled us both into his arms like he didn't know whether to cry or scream. He kissed our foreheads one by one, holding us so close it felt like he was trying to imprint the moment on his soul.

"My babies. All three of y'all. A table for three turning into a table for five. Damn."

Uncle Junebug sat up, looking around. "So who bringing the twins next year?"

Zaire shouted, "Not it!" and knocked over his water. "I'll babysit, but I don't do diapers."

Everyone cracked up again, and for a minute, it was just noise and love and Black joy wrapped up in all its loud, messy glory.

Later, we slipped out onto the porch, the stars sprawled above us like they had something to say. Symere stood between us, arms around our shoulders. Maleia leaned into him. I leaned into her.

"This life," he said quietly, "ain't just something we built. It's something we protect. Something we honor."

"Always," I said.

"Forever," Maleia added.

My hand rested on my belly, and hers mirrored the motion. The babies hadn't even come yet, but they were already surrounded by legacy.

Symere kissed the top of both our heads. "From a table for three to a table for five."

acknowledgments

To my beta readers: y'all were in my messages wilding. Talking about cold showers, pacing in your kitchens, and reading scenes twice just to make sure you *really* saw what you thought you saw. You helped shape this book with honesty, chaos, and love. I appreciate every one of you.

To the ARC readers: you didn't just read this story, you *carried* it. You shared it, screamed about it, and made sure it found the exact readers who needed it. Thank you for hyping this on your pages, your group chats, and your book worlds.

And to my loyal Patreon members, Lena and Tiffany, the ones who stay, support, and ride for me every step: I see you. I value you. This book is just as much yours as it is mine. Thank you. All of you. For believing in messy love, beautiful heat, and stories that don't apologize for either.

To the Discord girlies: Thank you for always listening to my crazy thoughts, thank you for helping me by listening to me talk about this book, and giving me pointers. I love y'all. Y'all are the real MVPs.

To my fiancé: Thank you for always supporting me and help me through this book. I love you.

about the author

C.M. Campbell is a stay-at-home mom, lifelong reader, and storyteller who finally decided to take the leap in 2025. Though she's been writing for years, it wasn't until recently that she gave herself permission to treat it like more than just a dream.

For her, stories have always been a  place of healing—a way to find light in the shadows and softness after survival. Through every character and chapter, she writes with purpose: to honor Black love, growth, and legacy. Her books are rooted in real emotion, rich intimacy, and the quiet power of choosing yourself.

When she's not writing, you can find her in the thick of motherhood, curled up with a book, or building the kind of life she used to only imagine.

also by cm campbell

Colliding Into His Arms

In My Rhythm

Beneath His Stetson

The Last Stream

Table For Three